# OLD WITCH
## and the
### POLKA·DOT RIBBON

*To our son, David*

# and the POLKA·DOT RIBBON

By Wende and Harry Devlin

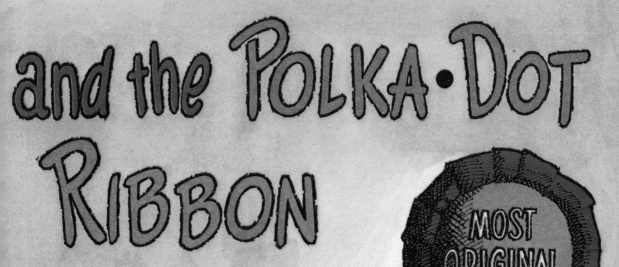

Parents' Magazine Press • New York

Howling winds sent branches scraping against the windows and shutters of the old Jug and Muffin Tearoom. Rain splashed and sudden lightning made wild shadows on the flapping shingles. It was a terrible morning.

"What a beautiful morning," said Old Witch, who watched the storm from her quilt-covered bed. With a leap she was out of her quilts and into her high-buttoned shoes. A quick look in the mirror told her that her hair was a fright, so she grabbed her pointed old hat and jammed it down on her head. She made a face in the mirror and slid down the bannister to the kitchen.

With a great deal of noise, she crashed into the kitchen door.

"Bats!" she said.

In the kitchen, very busy with stirring and pour-
ing, were Nicky and his mother, who owned the
tearoom. Old Witch had lived in the attic ever since
that day they had awakened her from a long sleep
in the chimney. When she felt like it, Old Witch
helped with the cooking.

"What's cooking?" said Old Witch, glaring at all
the activity.

Nicky's mother carefully explained about the contest. Oldwick needed a new bandstand and the townspeople agreed that a carnival, with a cake baking contest, would be a fine way to raise money.

"A new bandstand!" Old Witch screeched. "What's wrong with the old one? It's got everything —spiders, mice, cobwebs and bats."

Nicky thought the best way to answer Old Witch was to invite her to the carnival. "You'll have a wonderful time," he said. "And if you like, you may enter the contest, but Mrs. Butterbean *always* wins the first prize at every cake contest."

Old Witch's answer was a snort as she perched herself high on a shelf to tease the cooks. She cackled as she told Nicky that she was going to sprinkle sand on his sugar cookies.

Nicky's mother finally lost her patience as Old Witch knocked a can of pepper into her lemon icing. Between sneezes she ordered the old trouble-maker out of the kitchen.

"A wart pox on both of you—on carnivals—on bandstands—on lemon cakes!" She stopped long enough to make a face which was rather frightening on top of her own face. Then grabbing her broom she sailed out of the house to the top of the black walnut tree to sulk and mutter little rhymes like this:

*Toil and trouble*
*For Old Witch,*
*I hope they all*
*Get wild oak itch.*

She banged a black walnut with her fist. Her eyes
suddenly lit up.

*A big green moon,*
*A toad's blue eyes.*
*I'll make nut cake*
*And win first prize.*

Old Witch stayed up in the tree until Nicky and his mother left for the carnival. Back in the kitchen, she tied on a great flowered apron. Pans rattled, flour flew. A trip to the cellar brought long forgotten spices to mingle with pumpkin and sugar. In no time the cake was frosted, covered with a checkered napkin, and packed in a basket.

Basket, broom and Old Witch were soon on the
way to Oldwick.

There in the village square, flags were flying over striped tents and all around was a wonderful holiday spirit.

Old Witch made her way through the crowds to
the main tent. Sometimes her nose barely reached
the table tops and once she almost had it caught in
the cider press at the apple exhibit.

Now, at last, Old Witch entered her cake in the contest and stopped to look about.

Would the judges dare to choose someone else's cake?

She hopped up on the display table to get a better look. Her hat accidentally fell into a large white whipped cream cake, but she smoothed it over nicely with her broom. She tasted the strawberry cake—now the banana—and finally she dipped into a chocolate square.

"Tasty," she squawked, "very tasty."

She scurried out to a table by the entrance. She peeked out from under the tablecloth and saw the elegant Mrs. Butterbean coming down the path. While her chauffeur carried a tall coconut cake, Mrs. Butterbean carried her nose high in the air.

"Hush, now!" she whispered loudly. "No one must know that a famous baker makes these for me. By hook or by crook, the Butterbeans always win."

Old Witch became very angry when she heard this.

"Bats, crickets and snakes' knees." She cracked her knuckles and popped her eyes. Imagine anyone cheating—other than herself, of course.

Mrs. Butterbean put the cake on the table just above Old Witch's head and turned to say good-bye.

Carefully, Old Witch crept out and removed her
hat. She slid the coconut cake onto her head, jammed
on her hat and coasted off on her broomstick high
above the tent tops.

As she circled overhead, she was somewhat pleased
to hear angry voices and cries of outrage.

The sun sank like a pink ball in a lavender sky and Mrs. Butterbean still searched wildly behind bushes, under tents and among small boys.

Sometimes there seemed to be a faint cackling in the wind and a light rain of something that looked like coconut as night came over the carnival.

A bit later, Nicky and his mother arrived home.

Old Witch sat rocking by the fireplace. She turned her back on them and pretended to have no interest in who might have won the baking contest.

"Old Witch, dear," said Nicky's mother, "Nicky won in the children's contest. But the most shocking thing happened. They think a cow got loose in the cake tent and Mrs. Butterbean's cake completely disappeared."

"Mrs. Butterbean's cake disappeared?" said Old Witch, looking at the ceiling. "There was a strong wind today."

She rose and glared at them.

"What about my magic nut cake?"

"You won a ribbon for the most original,"
Nicky's mother laughed.

"The judges thought it had a haunting flavor,"
Nicky added and pinned a polka-dot ribbon on her
cape.

"Old Witch, what are all those crumbs on your cape?" Nicky asked.

"Just a little dust from dancing," she muttered.

Dodging away, Old Witch made her way noisily up the attic stairs, clacking her wooden heels at each landing. She leaned over the railing.

"And no blasted dinner for me tonight. I'm feeling delicate."

"For goodness' sakes." Nicky's mother brushed up the floor with her fireside broom.

"I smell coconut, Nicky. Do you think Old Witch could have . . .?"

Nicky sniffed. "Our Old Witch?" he said, looking at the attic. "Of course not!"

And upstairs Old Witch crept under her quilt.
"Jumping Jehosaphat! I had no idea how much
trouble it was to enter a cake baking contest—or how
filling." She winked at her polka-dot ribbon and
cackled goodnight to the black crow on her window-
sill. Then putting her hat over her face, she fell into
a deep, sweet sleep.